Winners Don't Whine and Whiners Don't Win!

CW00661602

Published by

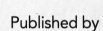

NATIONAL CENTER for
YOUTH ISSUES

www.ncyi.org

Duplication and Copyright

No part of this publication may be reproduced, stored in a retrieval system or transmitted in any form by any means, electronic, mechanical, photocopy, recording or otherwise without prior written permission from the publisher except for all worksheets and activities which may be reproduced for a specific group or class. Reproduction for an entire school or school district is prohibited.

NATIONAL CENTER for **YOUTH ISSUES**

P.O. Box 22185
Chattanooga, TN 37422-2185
423.899.5714 • 866.318.6294
fax: 423.899.4547 • www.ncyi.org

ISBN: 978-1-937870-41-6 $9.95
© 2016 National Center for Youth Issues, Chattanooga, TN
All rights reserved.
Written by: Julia Cook
Illustrations by: Anita DuFalla
Design by: Phillip W. Rodgers
Contributing Editor: Beth Spencer Rabon
Published by National Center for Youth Issues • Softcover
Printed at Starkey Printing, Chattanooga, Tennessee, U.S.A., July 2018

My name is
Wendell and
I LOVE to win…
at everything!

"**I WIN!** I'm smarter than you are!!"

"**I WIN!** NANA NANA BOO BOO!"

"**I WIN!** My score's higher than yours!"

"**I WIN!** I eat faster than you do!"

I love to **WIN!** I always want to be first.
And I love to get my way, because losing is the worst.

Speaking of "worst," today was the **WORST DAY EVER!**
This morning, my sister Eunice raced me to the kitchen table for breakfast. I lost, and she grabbed the box of Honey Busters and emptied it into her bowl!!

"GEEEEZE Eunice! I wanted some!!!
Why did you take it all? That's not fair!!!"

"Wendell…winners aren't whiners and whiners never win.
Today just isn't your day."

Then at school, we had a times table test and I finished first!

"**I WIN!**" I said.

"We'll see," said my teacher.

Turns out Gertie won because she had the most right answers.

"Wendell, winners don't whine and whiners never win. Today just isn't your day."

During lunch time, I raced Wilber in a pudding slurp contest…
and **I LOST!!!!**

"GEEEEZE! that's not fair!
My lid ripped when I tried to pull it off."

"Wendell…winners aren't whiners and whiners never win.
Today just isn't your day."

After school, I raced Eunice home from the bus stop. I always win when we race…but not today.

""Hey, no fair Eunice…my shoe fell off. GEEEEZE!"

"Wendell…winners aren't whiners and whiners never win.
Today just isn't your day."

Before I went to bed, I played cards with my mom.
We played fish…and she won. We played war…and she won.
But when we played concentration…**I WON!!!!**

"But Wendell, if you cheat to win, it's not really a win.

So actually, you lost."

"BUT MOM... I never win!! I've lost ALL DAY LONG! I lost at school and I lost at home!

I must be a loser.

I have **LOSER'S DISEASE!**

No matter what I do, I can't win Mom, GEEEEZE!"

"Wendell,
stop **WHINING!**
Your voice
hurts my ears!

It's like nails on a chalkboard!
And dry up those tears!

Whiners aren't winners
And winners don't whine.

You can't win at everything
all of the time."

"But Mom, today, I didn't win at anything. I didn't even beat Eunice home from the bus stop, and she runs about as fast as an ant!"

"Wendell, maybe today just wasn't your day.

No matter how hard you prepare, or how hard you work at things, or how hard you try to get your own way, you simply can't win <u>every</u> time.

Nobody can. And nobody should.

It's actually **GOOD** for you when you don't win sometimes."

"How is being a loser good for me?"

"Losing doesn't make you a loser...it makes you better. A person who wins every time forgets how to try, and then he stops being the best he can be.

Instead of being so focused on winning or losing, think about trying hard to do your best. Then if you do lose, at least you know that you gave it everything you had.

Besides, if you don't let yourself feel the pain of a loss once in a while, you'll never learn to truly appreciate what it feels like to win!"

"Losing doesn't make you a loser.
But how do you handle a loss?

Having the right **ATTITUDE**
is very important.

Cause you'll never
win every coin toss.

""But I HATE losing. GEEEEZE!"

*"I understand how you feel when you lose.
And I know why sometimes you whine.*

*You're probably hungry or tired or bored,
and you're needing somebody's time.*

*But whining isn't the answer either.
Instead, use your talking voice.*

*Then you will find that people will listen.
Whining's never the very best choice."*

"But I don't whine all of the time, Mom."

"Nope, but every time you lose,
"Wendell" morphs into
"**Wendell the Whiner**,"

and that drives everybody around you **NUTS! "**

"Life's not always about
WENDELL vs. the WORLD.
You need to learn to be part of a team.

*You might be good at one thing or another,
but you're not great at everything."*

*"If you can work well with others,
and be a part of something bigger than you,
then you'll really start to win at life,
and you'll be amazed at what you can do!"*

"Oh, and cheating to win is never a good thing.
A real win has to be true.

Having good character is a must.
In the end, a cheater will lose."

"And when you do win it's very important
to have a good attitude.
A winner that gloats or brags about things
is not a good winner…that's rude!

Instead, congratulate the efforts of others.
Having good character is a must.
And always remember how you felt,
the last time that you lost."

"But Mom…today I didn't win at anything! GEEEEZE!"

"What's that Wendell? When you use your **WHINY VOICE** I can't understand a word you are saying."

"I said, today I didn't win at **ANYTHING!**"

"Everyone has days like that.
You're going to be OK.
Just think about what I have told you.
TOMORROW'S A BRAND NEW DAY!

When you wake up tomorrow,
try out what I have said.
You'll start to realize that
there's a lot more to life,
than winning or feeling bad."

This morning, I raced Eunice to the table for breakfast. We tied! But in a way, we both won because my mom bought two boxes of Krispy Kritters!

At school, Gertie beat me again at our times table test.
We both got 100%, but she finished 2 seconds before I did.

I almost let out a "GEEEEZE!" but then I caught myself and said,
"Nice job, Gertie."

She better be ready tomorrow, because tonight I'm going
to **PRACTICE, PRACTICE, PRACTICE!!!!**

"Wilber and I pudding slurped during lunch again, and **I WON!**
This time I made sure I was careful when I pulled off my lid."

Inside my head I was thinking,
"NANA NANA BOO BOO, I'M BETTER THAN YOU ARE,"
but then I thought about what my mom told me.

"Nice effort!" I said.

"Thanks, Wendell!"

After school, I raced Eunice from the bus stop, but halfway to our house, she tripped on her shoe lace and bit the dust!

Instead of making her feel bad, I walked the rest of the way home with her.

Sometimes winning isn't the most important thing.

That night, Eunice and I teamed up
and played against my mom in concentration.

We beat her four times in a row!

Two brains really are better than one!

We made a great team!

"Today I had a
much better day,
and I didn't even **whine**.

Winners don't whine
and whiners don't win.
And I can't **WIN** all of the time."

"Wendell, it's time to take a bath and get ready for bed."

"Oh Mom, GEEEEZE!"
Come on…I'm not even tired.
Can't I stay up later tonight, pleasseeeeee?"

"What's that Wendell, I can't understand what you are saying."

"Mom, can I please stay up for just a little bit longer?"

Teaching Your Child to Be a WINNER at LIFE!

At a young age, children start to take an interest in what others around them are doing. They begin to compare themselves to other people, and they soon realize that winning brings rewards, and losing doesn't. This can sometimes lead to over-competitiveness. Competition isn't bad. Seeing what others are doing inspires us to try harder to improve, and improving leads to a gain in self-confidence. But when competitiveness spins out of control, a child may start to do anything (cheat, lie, steal, argue, change the rules, etc.) to win.

Here are a few tips to help your child become a true winner.

- Attitude is everything! How you respond to victory and defeat is how your child will learn to respond. If you act disappointed when your children perform poorly, or if you are constantly comparing their performances to others, your children will learn that they will only get your approval when they are better than everyone else. If a child is desperate for approval, he/she will try to win at all costs – or quit all together and begin searching elsewhere for value.

- Help your child understand that winning isn't everything. What is far more important is putting forth your best effort.

- Praise the specific effort. Don't just say good job! For example, say "Nice kick!," "Way to improve your score!" or "That section sounded amazing!"

- Explain the benefits of losing to your child. Losing makes you appreciate winning. If you win all the time, you won't have a reason to try hard to be your best. Losing makes you smarter and encourages you to become better prepared, etc.

- Encourage your child to play by the rules. A cheater is never a true winner.

- Help your child set goals that can improve his/her individual performance. Instead of competing against others, try to compete against yourself. "How many foul shots can I make in a row?"

- Switch to activities that focus on skill building as opposed to score keeping (biking, dancing, karate, etc.).

- Never tolerate poor sportsmanship. Win with appreciation and lose with dignity.

- If your child becomes very frustrated with his/her performance, give the child time to calm down and regroup. Then together create a plan that can help your child improve. (Private music lessons, extra batting practice throughout the week and before a game, positive self-talk, etc.).

- To win at life, a child must be able to both compete and collaborate. Teach your child the importance of being a good team player. Remember…There is no "I" in team!

- Remember, competition is important. Winning should feel triumphant, and losing should feel disappointing and encourage us all to work harder. If the two become the same, mediocrity takes over. We must teach our children to find that balance between competition and collaboration if we want them to win at life.

Stopping the WHINE!

Whining is not a conscious strategy, it is a learned behavior that is totally normal. Everyone whines at one time or another. That shrill, "nails on the chalkboard" sound expresses a loss of power that talking and crying just don't have.

Children often whine when they are tired, hungry, angry or bored. They have great expectations in life, and sometimes they just don't end up getting what they want. This makes a child feel powerless and disconnected. Sometimes whining works, and parents give in. Whining works! That's why kids do it!

Here are a few tips to stop the "WHINE"

- Try to figure out why your child is whining. Why does he/she feel out of control of the situation? Is he hungry? Is she tired? Is he bored because you have been shopping for three hours? Is she just venting? Finding out the reason and rectifying the situation is the first step.

- React in a positive way. "I know you are tired, but when you use your whiney voice I can't understand what you are saying. Tell me what you want in your talking voice."

- Don't give in! If you give into the whine, you are only encouraging your child to whine again in the future.

- When your child doesn't whine, thank them for using their talking voice.